Euclid Bunny Delivers the Mail

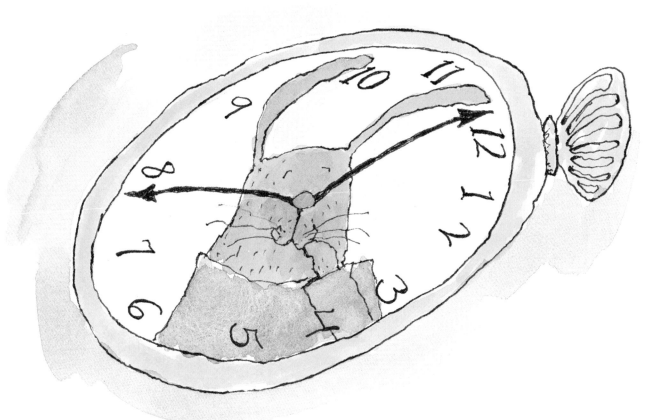

BRUCE KOSCIELNIAK

ALFRED A. KNOPF : NEW YORK

For Betty Lou Zajac

Day was breaking on the Barnyard post office.

All the chickens who deliver the Barnyard mail were down with the flu. And the post office was filled to the rafters with letters and packages waiting to be delivered.

"Whatever will we do?" groaned postmaster Bernie Bear.

"Pretend there's no mail?" sighed Fluffy Fowl.

"Let's call Euclid Bunny Speedy Delivery Service!" clucked Muffy Hen.

"Dial the number," said Bernie.

POSTMASTER B. BEAR

TELEPHONE

SERVICE WITH A SMILE

"Hello? Euclid Bunny? Bernie Bear here. We've got a little problem at the post office this morning. Can you help us?"

Quick as a bunny, Euclid was there.

"Here's the delivery route. Take this map. You should be back in three or four hours," said Bernie. "And make sure you get the out-of-town mail to the station for the three o'clock train. Got it?"

"I'm out of here," chimed the speedy bunny.

BARNYAF

BARNYARD
POST OFFICE

MOUSE
FIELD

BARNYARD RAILWAY
STATION
3 P.M. TRAIN

Bunny quick, Euclid loaded all the mail into his truck,
and off he went. First he stopped at the mouse field.

Then he sped through the cow pasture.

He breezed by the duck pond.

And skipped past the pig farm.
"What was that?" asked Penny Pig.

Then Euclid delivered all the mail for the deer and the moose.

This is too easy, he thought as he hopped about his business.

In a twitch he was scooting up to the squirrels' nest.

And down to the owls'.

"Yikes!" muttered Euclid, "there's the train for the out-of-town mail. I'd better step on it."

BARNYARD STATION →

← ROCKY MOUNTAINS POINTS WEST

TOOT TOOT

Euclid Bunny Speedy Service

And with the mail safely on the train, Euclid raced back to the Barnyard post office.

BARNYARD

"Uh-oh, something wrong? Am I late?" asked Euclid when he arrived. "You've only been gone twenty minutes," gruffed Bernie.

But something *was* wrong. Mortimer Moose had gotten a TV
that should have gone to Murray Mouse. Donny and Dotty Mouse
had gotten a refrigerator meant for Danny and Dorry Deer.

Scotty Squirrel had gotten Pomeroy Pig's golf clubs. Roland Reindeer
had gotten six hats addressed to Dubber and Dilly Duck's ducklings.

Percy Pig got Monty Moose's bath soap. And Durwin
Duck got a postcard from "Mom and Dad"—Betty and Bruno Bear.

Chloe Cow got someone's tiny tea service. And Olivia Owl
got Penny Pig's umbrella stand.

"Seems like you were a bit too hasty," growled
Bernie Bear. "Now what are we going to do?"
"Oooh, don't worry. I'll take care of it," said Euclid.

Bunny quick, he hopped around the Barnyard post office sorting the mail.

And when everything landed,

everyone had the right things.

"Call me if you ever need help again," said Euclid.
"Maybe," said Bernie. "Hey, wait a minute. There's a
letter here addressed to Euclid Bunny."

Dear Euclid,

We just got a call from Benny, the Barnyard Easter Bunny, who's down with the flu. Looks like you'll have to deliver the Barnyard Easter eggs this year, Sonny. So hotfoot it home and bring lots of eggs!

Love,
Granny Bunny

Euclid
Bunny
Barnyard Post Office

Quick as a bunny, Euclid was gone.

THIS IS A BORZOI BOOK PUBLISHED BY ALFRED A. KNOPF, INC.

Copyright © 1991 by Bruce Koscielniak

All rights reserved under International and Pan-American Copyright Conventions. Published in the United States
by Alfred A. Knopf, Inc., New York, and simultaneously in Canada by Random House of Canada Limited, Toronto.
Distributed by Random House, Inc., New York.

Book design by Mina Greenstein
Manufactured in the United States of America
2 4 6 8 10 9 7 5 3 1

Library of Congress Cataloging-in-Publication Data
Koscielniak, Bruce.
Euclid Bunny delivers the mail / by Bruce Koscielniak.
p.   cm. Summary: When the chickens who deliver the Barnyard mail come down with the flu,
postmaster Bernie Bear hires a speedy bunny to do the job, with humorous results.
ISBN 0-679-81069-2 (trade)   ISBN 0-679-91069-7 (lib. bdg.)
[1. Postal service—Letter carriers—Fiction. 2. Animals—Fiction.]   I. Title.   PZ7.K8523Eu 1991
[E]—dc20 90-4696 CIP AC